Journey to Nazgar's Fortress

A ROBO FORCE ADVENTURE

By Bill Chatham

Illustrated by
Juan Gimenez

Random House 🏠 New York

Copyright © 1985 CBS Inc. All rights reserved under International and Pan-American Copyright Conventions. Published in the United States by Random House, Inc., New York, and simultaneously in Canada by Random House of Canada Limited, Toronto. Library of Congress Catalog Card Number: 84-62071   ISBN: 0-394-87175-8   Manufactured in the United States of America   1 2 3 4 5 6 7 8 9 0

The beautiful city of Celestia lay peacefully in the rose and orange of the blossoming sunrise. But Dr. Richard Fury, the planet Zeton's greatest living scientist, knew no peace as he sat in his laboratory in the Fortress of Steele, rubbing his weary eyes. He had worked all night on the single most important project of his career: a plan to destroy Celestia's most dreaded enemy, Nazgar the Invincible!

Nazgar was a cruel, wicked warlord whose human brain was encased in a powerful computerized robot body. His sinister goal was to enslave the peaceful people of Zeton, using his army of evil robots.

"Our project must succeed—it must!" Dr. Fury mumbled as he worked. Throughout the city, Zeton's other top scientists were also at work, alone and in secret, for Nazgar's spies were everywhere!

Not far away Nazgar sat in the red glow of the central intelligence monitor in his own fortress. "The fools!" he cried. "Do Fury and those other dolts who call themselves scientists really think they can keep their plans from me? My spy network is the best in the universe!"

"You are indeed wise!" crooned Hun-Dred, Nazgar's right-hand robot. "How clever of you to uncover their latest plot!"

"But I need more information!" boomed Nazgar. "Dr. Fury seeks a rare Zeton element in his efforts to destroy me. Whatever it is, *we* must find it first!"

Back at the Fortress of Steele, Councilwoman Deena Strong was paying Dr. Fury an early-morning visit.

"Any progress, Doctor?" she asked.

"Yes—I've got it!" shouted Dr. Fury. He thrust his notes into Deena's hands.

"Got what, Dad?" called Mark Fury, dashing in with his loyal robot friend, Maxx Steele.

"The rare element I need to fuel my de-Nazgarator," his father explained. "It's called ryton!"

"Where can we find ryton?" asked Mark.

Dr. Fury fed some figures into his computer, waited, and then—

"Oh, no!" he cried. "Look at this!"

Mark, Deena, and Maxx gasped.

"Dr. Fury!" cried Deena. "You mean the only place this element exists is—"

"Yes," moaned Dr. Fury. "In the dead volcano of Nazgar's fortress!"

"I don't suppose he'd be a good neighbor and lend us a cup," joked Maxx.

"Be serious," said Mark. "We'll just have to go in and get it ourselves. Maxx, round up the rest of the Robo Force crew— we've got work to do!"

"I'm coming too!" insisted Deena.

Mark frowned. "Deena, I don't think—"

"Good! Don't think! Just grab your keys to the Command Patroller and let's go!"

Soon Mark, Deena, and the Robo Force were speeding away from Celestia over deadly deserts and boiling seas. Suddenly the twisted peak of Nazgar's fortress came into view.

"My information disk is picking up a definite crack in a quadrant of their force field," said S.O.T.A. "Perhaps we can enter through there."

"Good work!" said Mark. He steered the Command Patroller into a crater a few hundred meters below the fortress. "Sentinel, please stand guard over our vehicles. The rest of you come with me."

As they passed through the force field, S.O.T.A. created interference to shield them from Nazgar's radar. Then Coptor spun his propeller and began to tunnel into the ancient volcanic rock.

"That's using your head!" said Wrecker, and with his atomic-powered jackhammer, he helped Coptor dig to Nazgar's mines.

S.O.T.A. switched to long-distance hearing. "I just hope we can accomplish our mission undetected," he said.

"Here's our plan," said Mark. "We'll each search a tunnel and then meet back here in fifteen minutes."

Halfway down one tunnel, Deena discovered some mining equipment. When she kicked at the surrounding rubble, a strange blue glint caught her eye. She knelt to examine the rocks at her feet.

"Looking for something, Ms. Strong?" boomed a voice from behind her, and a cold steel gripper clamped down on her shoulder. It was Hun-Dred!

As he dragged her away to the upper levels of the fortress, Deena secretly sent out an S.O.S. by pressing a button on the transmitter hidden in her belt. Would Mark Fury and the Robo Force receive her signal in time?

"How lovely to see you, Ms. Strong," said Nazgar as Hun-Dred brought her into the command chamber. "Please answer a few questions for me about Dr. Fury's work. I hear he doesn't like me."

"Too much time around these vicious vacuum cleaners has warped your brain, Nazgar!" cried Deena as Vulgar strapped her into a massive electronic chair. "I won't talk!"

"You won't have to," Nazgar replied calmly, flipping a switch. "This new toy of mine will read your thoughts for me!"

The machine whirred into operation. Would Deena's helpless mind reveal all of Dr. Fury's secrets?

But the machine's monitor showed nothing!

"What's wrong with this worthless piece of junk?" Nazgar shouted. He whirled around to glare at Deena.

Her hands were clenched, but her eyes were closed and her face had the gentle look of someone who was dreaming peacefully. She had made her mind a total blank! As a little girl, Deena had learned this ancient trick from her grandmother, one of Zeton's first explorers to other galaxies.

"We'll have to think of something else!" Nazgar said irritably.

But as he spoke, explosions rocked the entrance to the fortress!

"It must be Fury—and his oil-can army!" cried Nazgar, checking his security monitor. "Quick, Vulgar! Call the others! Hun-Dred, stay here and guard this silly woman!"

Soon Nazgar's robots and the Robo Force were locked in battle at the fortress doors.

"Take that, you rusty eggbeater!" shouted Enemy as his chest compartment opened to blast Coptor with twin lasers. But Coptor's propellers whisked him out of danger just in time—and he sent Enemy an answering laser blast.

Meanwhile, Cruel and Wrecker fought head-to-head as Nazgar screamed orders from the safety of his command post.

But where were Mark and Maxx?

"Well, if it isn't my old pal Hun-Dred," said Maxx as he and Mark charged into the command chamber. For a moment Hun-Dred stood frozen in surprise. It was all the time Maxx needed to fire his laser pistol and deal Hun-Dred a stunning blow.

"Great work!" shouted Mark. He freed Deena and headed for the door. "Keep him busy till we get out of here!"

Suddenly Hun-Dred snapped up his weapon hood and aimed his pop-up lasers at Maxx's chest. But Maxx dodged—and used his hand laser to send Hun-Dred spinning.

"We'll have to finish this dance some other time," Maxx said, and dashed out.

"How can I face Dad without the ryton?" said Mark as the weary crew arrived back at the Fortress of Steele. To make matters worse, once inside they found Nazgar speaking over the telecommunicator.

"Dr. Fury, we enjoyed your group's little visit," said Nazgar, "and we finally figured out what they were after. I'm afraid your precious ryton is now packed and on its way to a distant asteroid. It would take Mark Fury and the Robo Force two thousand years to find it!" Nazgar's evil laugh faded hauntingly as the transmission died away.

Mark groaned. "Looks like that bottled brain and his hardware hooligans have beaten us at last!"

"Don't be so sure," said Deena. "I had just discovered Nazgar's ryton mine when I was kidnapped. But I did manage to pick up a souvenir for the doctor." Smiling, she pulled a strange blue rock from a secret compartment in her belt.

"Ryton ore!" cried Dr. Fury.

"Nice going!" said Maxx.

"But that's not enough to fuel the de-Nazgarator, is it?" asked Mark.

The brilliant doctor was too busy scribbling notes to answer. But then he smiled.

"With the help of Zeton's other top scientists," he said excitedly, "there's a chance I can use this sample to duplicate ryton in the lab!" Dr. Fury was cheerful now—even laughing—as Mark, Maxx, and Deena left him to his work.

"This brings to mind an ancient proverb from a distant galaxy," said Maxx. "I believe it goes something like this: 'He who laughs last laughs best.'"

"Then I think we've got some side-splitting adventures ahead of us," said Mark, laughing, as he and Deena each put a friendly arm on Maxx's metallic shoulders.